For
My
Father

First published 2007 as *Wendel's Workshop*
by Macmillan Children's Books
This edition published 2019 by Macmillan's Children's Books
an imprint of Pan Macmillan
20 New Wharf Road, London N1 9RR
Associated companies throughout the world
www.panmacmillan.com

ISBN 978-1-5290-1754-0

Text and illustrations copyright © Chris Riddell 2007, 2015

The right of Chris Riddell to be identified as the
author and illustrator of this work has been asserted
by him in accordance with the Copyright,
Designs and Patents Act 1988.

1 3 5 7 9 8 6 4 2

A CIP catalogue record for this book is
available from the British Library.

Printed in China

Chris Riddell

Wendel
and the
Robots

Macmillan Children's Books

WENDEL was
an inventor.

Sometimes his inventions
worked perfectly,
and sometimes
they didn't.

When they didn't, Wendel
just threw them away and
started again.

Wendel invented all day and into the night. Sometimes he was so busy inventing he forgot to go to bed.

And he never had time to tidy up.

Wendel's workshop became untidier . . .

and untidier . . .

and UNTIDIER.

"I need some help," said Wendel to himself.

So Wendel invented a robot.

CLUNK! CLUNK! CLUNK!

"I'll call you Clunk," said Wendel.

Clunk set to work tidying Wendel's workshop.

He made the bed . . .

folded the clothes . . .

and mopped the floor.

"Oh dear," said Wendel.

Clunk tried harder.

He put the teacups in
the sock drawer . . .

and filled the
laundry basket
with umbrellas.

"This isn't working,"
said Wendel.

So he threw
Clunk down the
rubbish chute . . .

CLUNK!

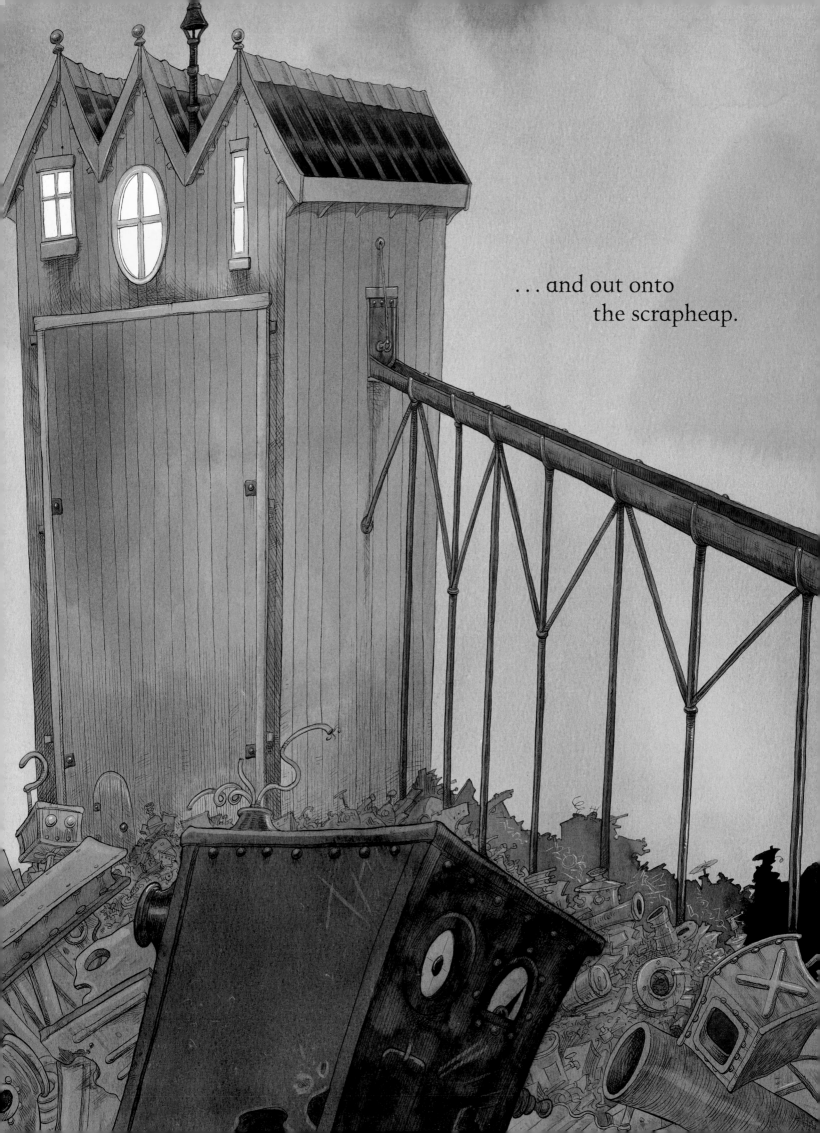

. . . and out onto
the scrapheap.

Inside the workshop,
Wendel was inventing
a new robot.

He worked all night . . .

and into the morning.

At last it was finished.

"I'll call you the Wendelbot," said Wendel.
"Tidy!" said the Wendelbot, its red eyes glowing. "Tidy!"
And it set to work.

The Wendelbot worked perfectly.
Wendel was very pleased.

But the Wendelbot didn't stop. Its red eyes glowed as it unmade the bed into a neat bundle, and crushed the teacups to a tidy pile of powder.

"Tidy!" the Wendelbot said as it shredded the umbrellas, and flattened the laundry basket. "Tidy!" Soon everything was neat and tidy.

All except one thing . . .

"Tidy!" cried the Wendelbot as it chased Wendel round the workshop.

"He-e-e-e-lp!" squeaked Wendel as he shot down the rubbish chute . . .

. . . and out onto the scrapheap.

Then, from quite
close by, Wendel
heard a clunk.

CLUNK!

"I'm SO pleased to see you!"
said Wendel.

From inside the workshop,
the noise of the Wendelbot's
hammering and bashing grew
louder and louder.

"We need some help," said Wendel,
"but all we've got is rubbish!"
Clunk reached down and handed
Wendel an interesting
piece of scrap.

Wendel smiled. And then he began to invent.

All day and into the
night, Wendel and Clunk
were hard at work.

As the sun rose, the hammering and bashing from
Wendel's workshop stopped.

"Workshop tidy!" said the Wendelbot.
It turned its glowing red eyes towards the window.
"NOW, TIDY WORLD!"

The Wendelbot strode across the workshop and threw open the door.

"Good morning," said Wendel.

The Wendelbot's eyes glowed red.
"Tidy!" it said.

"Untidy! Untidy!" Wendel and his robot
helpers shouted as they ran inside.

"TIDY!" cried the Wendelbot,
lumbering after them.

But the robots were too quick for it.

The Wendelbot's eyes glowed brighter and brighter as Wendel's workshop grew untidier and untidier.

"Ti-i-ide . . .   Ti-i-i . . . d-eeeeee!   TI-I-I . . . D-E-E-E!"

When the dust had settled, Wendel sighed.
"Now we'll have to tidy up again," he said.
"But not too much this time."

All the
robots helped . . .

in their different ways.

Not everything worked
perfectly . . .

but Wendel didn't mind.
He just smiled, patched
this, mended that, and
made adjustments
here and there.

But there was one thing he didn't do . . .

Wendel NEVER threw anything on the scrapheap again.